He Felt Unwell
(So He Wrote This)

Manufactured in the United States of America

ISBN: 978-0-578-64480-6

Formatting, illustrations, and cover design
by Alexandra Lenihan

for Brian

Hello.

I am a child
who happens
to also be
a twisted, stressed,
depressed
adult.

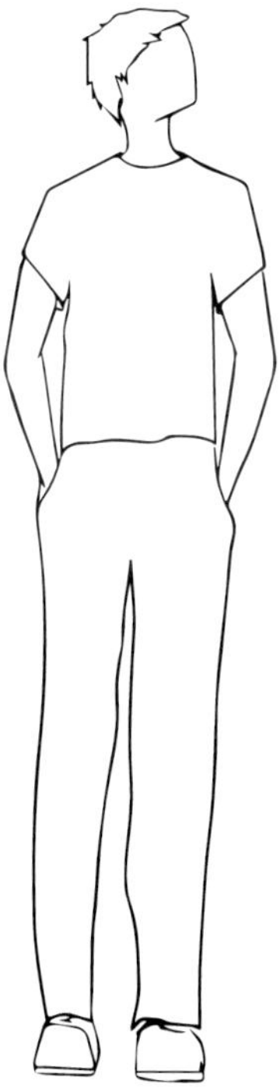

Poetry

is making
music
with your words.

It’s crafting
pain
into a song
that one day
you
may dance to.

They make you think your life
should read just like a book,

with feelings neatly plotted out,
    your Grief and Joy,
    your Love, your Doubt,
all caged in separate chapters.

But take a look inside your head,
see pages bleed into each other.
Some are torn, some pieced together,
the rest a jumbled mess.

Burn the book they write of you.
Breathe in your fumes
of chaos.

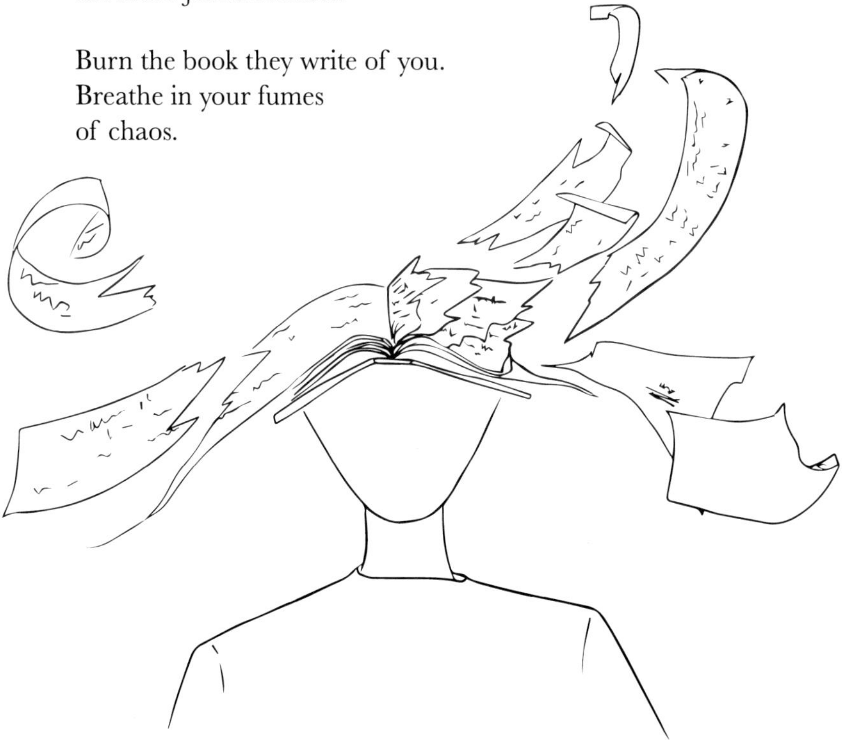

I hope the caterpillars
beneath my tongue

will one day flit
and fly away

and bring some color
to this world.

These words,

they beat like butterflies

circling my head,

begging to be written down,

yearning to be read.

My biggest fear

is drowning
in a sea

where I can stand,
should stand,
but for the life of me
cannot.

I feel
naked
on this
page.
Shield
your
eyes!
These
words,
they
bear
my soul,
the private
parts of me.

Be proud! says my brain. *You shouldn't be sad!*
You're the best prisoner that I've ever had!

- my brain is my warden

Growing up
I didn't play

hopscotch,

horse,

or kids croquet.

No,
growing up
my go-to game
was hiding
overwhelming

shame.

Spill your guts she said,
only to scream
and turn green
with pure dread
the second
I sliced
myself open.

-honesty

Maybe if I walk around with this

painted, happy face, these vibrant clothes,

this silly nose, they won't see my sadness.

My best friend? Well, his name is Doubt.
He likes to kick and scream and shout,
inside my head, in quiet rooms.
I've never known sweet Solitude.

Doubt won't let me. He's always there
to distract, confuse, and pull my hair,
to punch my gut and stomp my toes.
He fills me up with dread and woes.

Then just don't let him, you might say.
Pack your bags! Just run away!
It's not that easy, trust, I've tried.
He says the only way is...

...die.

And I won't do that! I can't! You hear?
My other friend, she's...Persevere.

I feel too
in my body,
claustrophobic
in this skin
that once could breathe
but now feels taut
like leather.

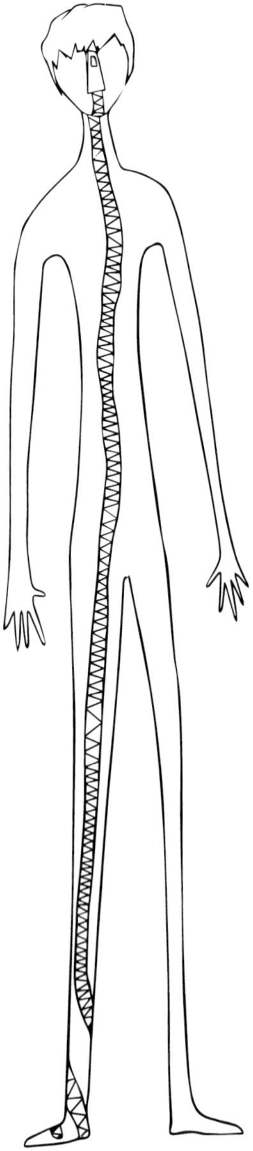

I fear my future

only because

of

how easy it was to convince myself I don't have one.

When you fear
the outside world
you tell yourself the closet
in which you cower
is not a closet,
but a palace.

You convince yourself
that a palace is a home,
lovely and lavish,
with lots of room
and light
and air to breathe.

Desperate to forget
that in reality,
you are curled up
on the floor
in the pitch-black
slowly suffocating.

Give up. You've lost.
The darkness cries,
flicking his tongue
and spewing his lies.

I've gobbled you up.
There's nowhere to run.
I've stomped out your flame,
extinguished the sun.

But now I can't see!
I say with a rumble,
gripping and tripping
and starting to tumble.

My breath gets heavy.
My knees go weak.
And just at that moment
I hear someone speak!

A familiar voice,
it cuts through the black.
I'm here! he says,
I'll help bring you back!

I follow the voice
to a door made of
light.
It opens and shines
and two arms hold me
tight.

I've got you now.
You can open your eyes.
Take in the sun
and the crystal clear skies.

Wow! I say,
with a rubber band smile.
I turn to the boy,
Can we stay awhile?

I have an endless hunger
for your licorice lips,
for those green grape eyes,
for my hands on your hips.

Quench my thirst
with a sip from your soul.
Slip off those jeans.
Let me fill up my bowl.

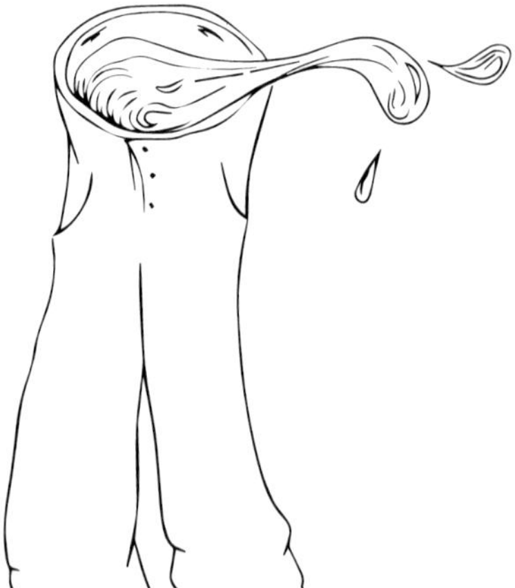

I am

the dream

to wean

you off

your nightmare.

I, for two decades,
built walls and tall towers

to contain my shame
and hide my desires.

Only to watch them
collapse into rubble,

the second your stubble
grazed my lips.

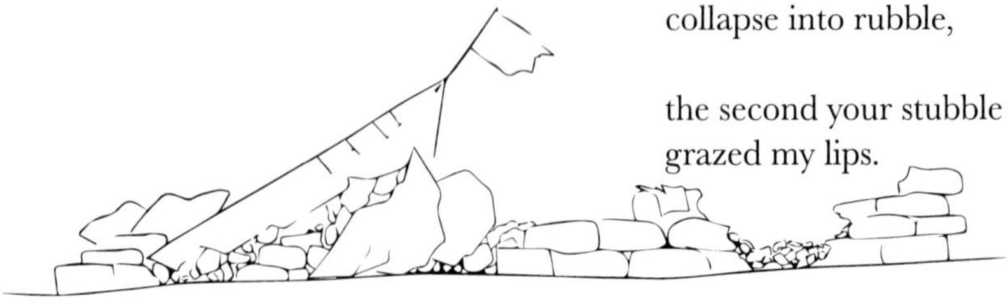

The freedom you'll feel

breaking out from your cage

far outweighs

all that comfortable fear.

I had a roommate growing up.
We went everywhere together,
did everything together,
shared our thoughts,
our feelings,

a body.

When it got too cramped,
he forced my hand.
So finally, I

moved out.

What do I do you ask?

I sit at a desk
from nine till five,
daydreaming of his smile,

crunching numbers only
to distract myself

from the distance,
from the breaths I take
of this air

that is not his.

-fire me

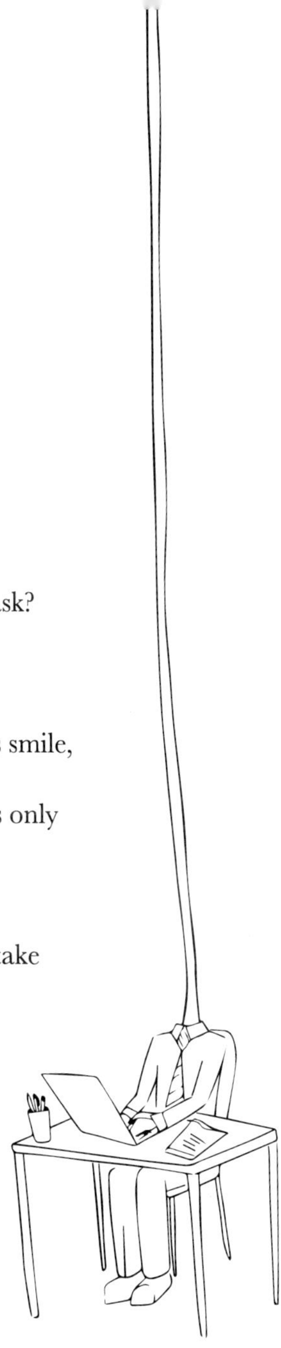

You move me

like the moon

pulls the sea.

In order to be free
I had to kill
that other me
with my bare hands.

Let us bow our heads
in silence
for the man
you always thought
I'd be.

Although you grieve,
I know you'll make
your peace
with this
new me.

They asked

at the Old Friends Q&A,

What happened to that other you?

And I replied,

He died.

I am haunted by the g h o s t of me.

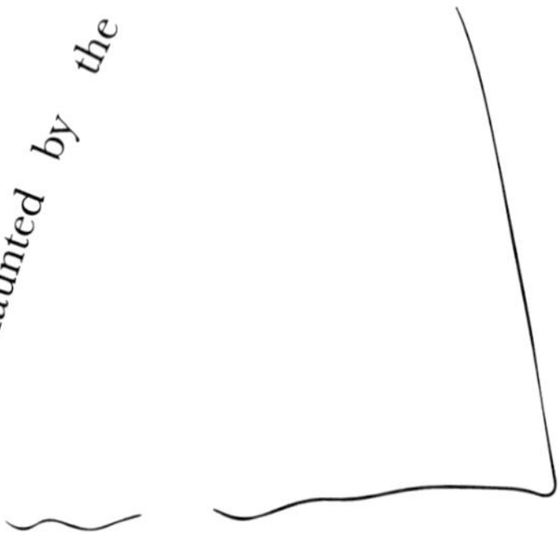

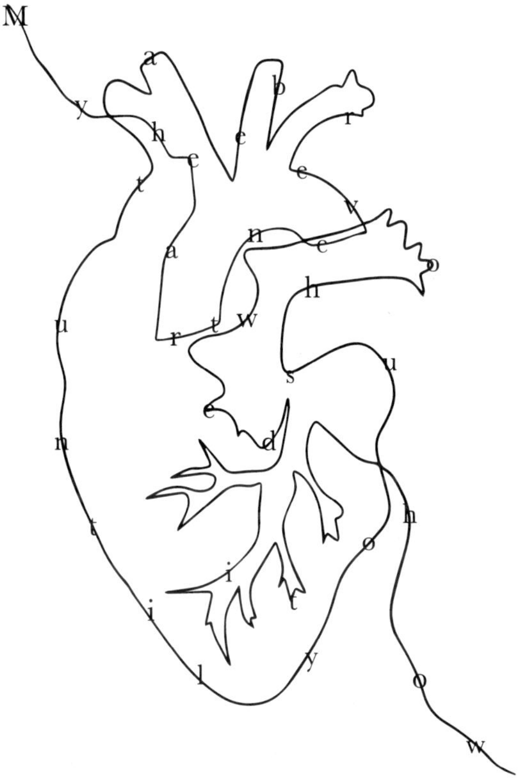
My heart never beat until you showed it how

Like a moth to a flame,
I am drawn to you.

Blissfully unafraid
of worshipping your warmth.

I was never one
to become
obsessed.

Yet here I lie
in this empty bed,
writhing in pain
at your silence.

Put me out
of my misery.

Tell me
where you are,
and who you're with,
and what you're doing
is a waste of time
'cause I'm not there.

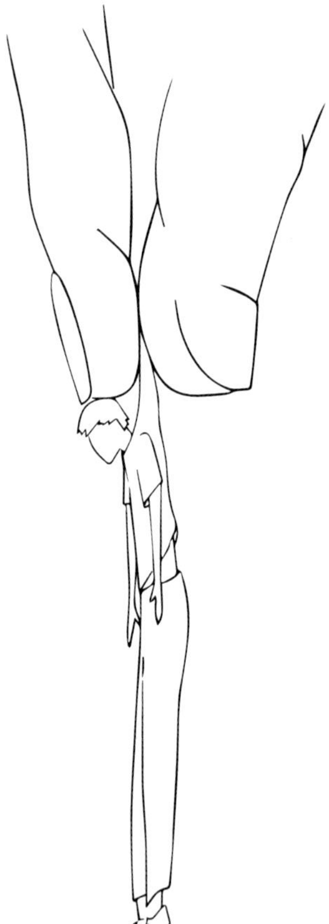

You lift me up and hold me
tight.
You tell me that I feel so light.
And I don't say
how it's the doubt
that's hollowed out

my bones.

You dipped
your loving words

in poison,

then
fed them to me.

-betrayal is a slow demise

Darling,

count your blessings.

Without me,
see,
you've got none.

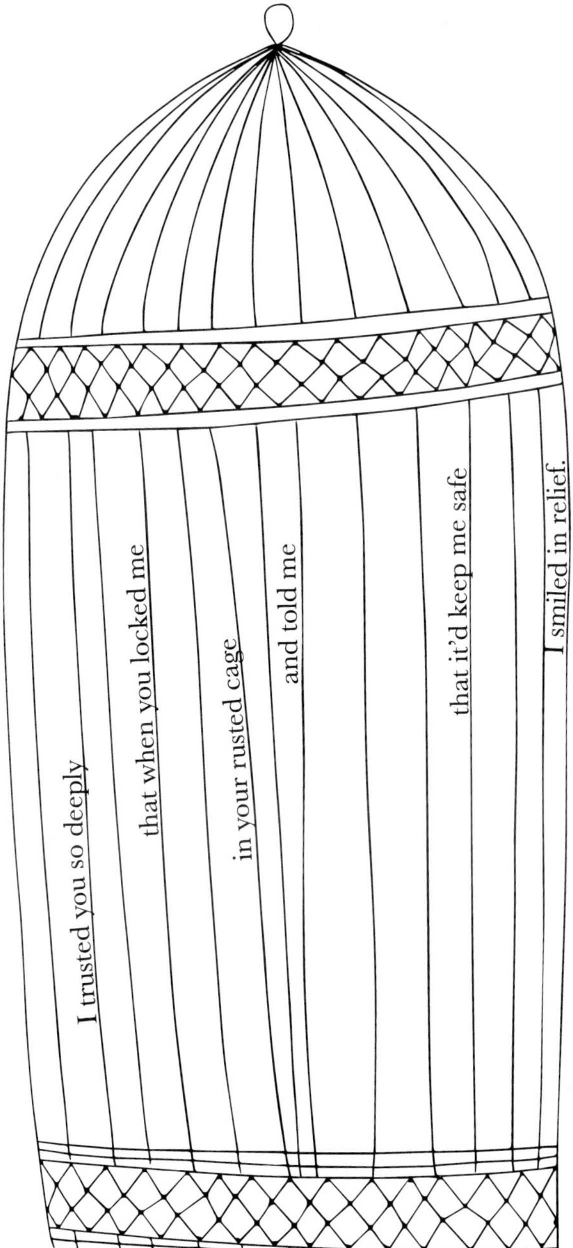
I trusted you so deeply
that when you locked me
in your rusted cage
and told me
that it'd keep me safe
I smiled in relief.

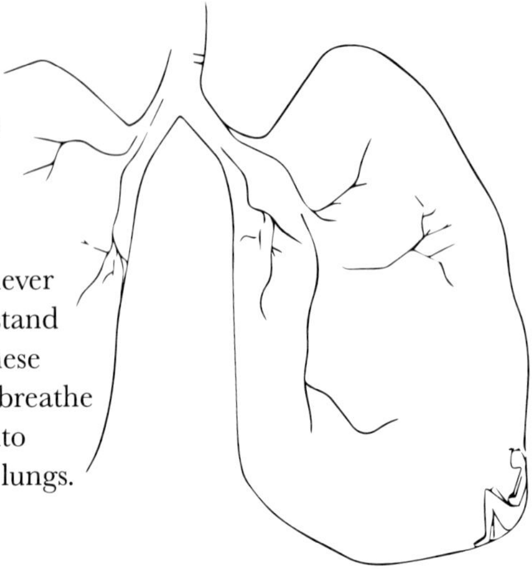

The
tragic
truth
is that
you'll never
understand
how these
poems breathe
life into
my lungs.

I think

deep down

you always hoped

I would drown,

so you never
taught me
how to swim.

Well, sorry dear

but I'm still here,
swimming laps

'cause I went
and taught

myself.

As we waded through the sea, I wrapped your hands

behind my head and said,

Go ahead. Drown your sorrows.

No, you did not die,
but I still watched
the bright light
slowly
slip out
from your eyes,
and be eaten
by the night.

You say you don't know
how you fell out of love,
but I watched
as you willingly
dove off the edge,
landing softly
into someone else's arms.

You wouldn't meet
my shattered stare.

Those downcast eyes,
they killed me.

Did your eyes even sting
when you chopped up
my heart
like an onion?

How did I feel
between your fingers?
Those coarse,
crushed up pieces
of my soul
you sprinkled
on your dinner.

I once held a dream
in my hands.
This beautiful surprise,
like a rare butterfly,
resting on my thumb.

I was so in love,
so captivated,
by the gleam of this dream,
that I wasn't prepared
when it flew through the air
and took all my hope
along with it.

You tied me up,
and struck your match,
and set our dream on fire.

I think you liked
to watch me
watch it
burn.

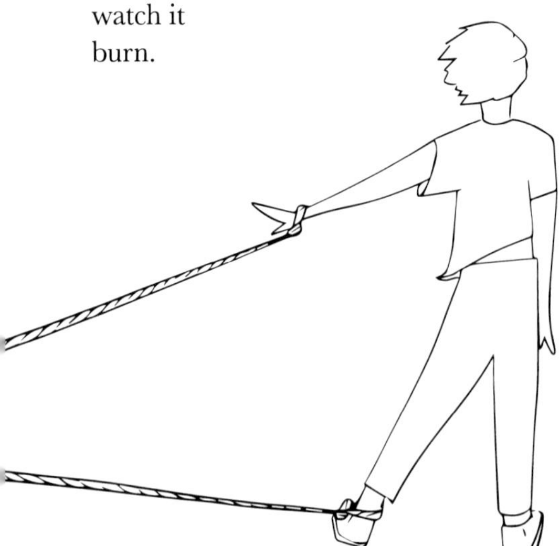

When your world burns to the ground,
they will stand above you as you
sink like quicksand in the ash.
Just rise they will say,
as if you are a child playing
in a pile of leaves.
It's easy they will assure,
as if you could just stand and
brush the gashes off your knees.
Can they not see
that you have nothing?
That you no longer have a clue
how to do
a single thing?
That when you breathe
you choke on smoke
and cannot see,
for toxic tears
still sting your eyes?

Ask them,
how does a phoenix rise
before it's grown its wings?
But you don't have time they will argue.
But they are wrong.
Time is all you have.
So you will take your time,
and lick your wounds,
and mourn your losses.
Learn all the lessons that
needed to be taught.
Then,
when you are finally ready,
you will not rise,
but hobble to your feet,
and bravely
trudge on.

You washed your sheets

and with them went

my scent

I left
on your pillow.

Sometimes I wish the world
forced us to wear
our fears and our flaws
like tattoos on our skin.
So on days we feel lonely,
we may walk through a crowd
and realize
we are not alone
at all.

When I die, I'd like to be planted as a willow tree.
So I may stretch my limbs up high,
and maybe this time touch the sky.
Then finally, I might feel free
of all my life's anxiety.
With up the only place to go
and nothing left to do but grow.

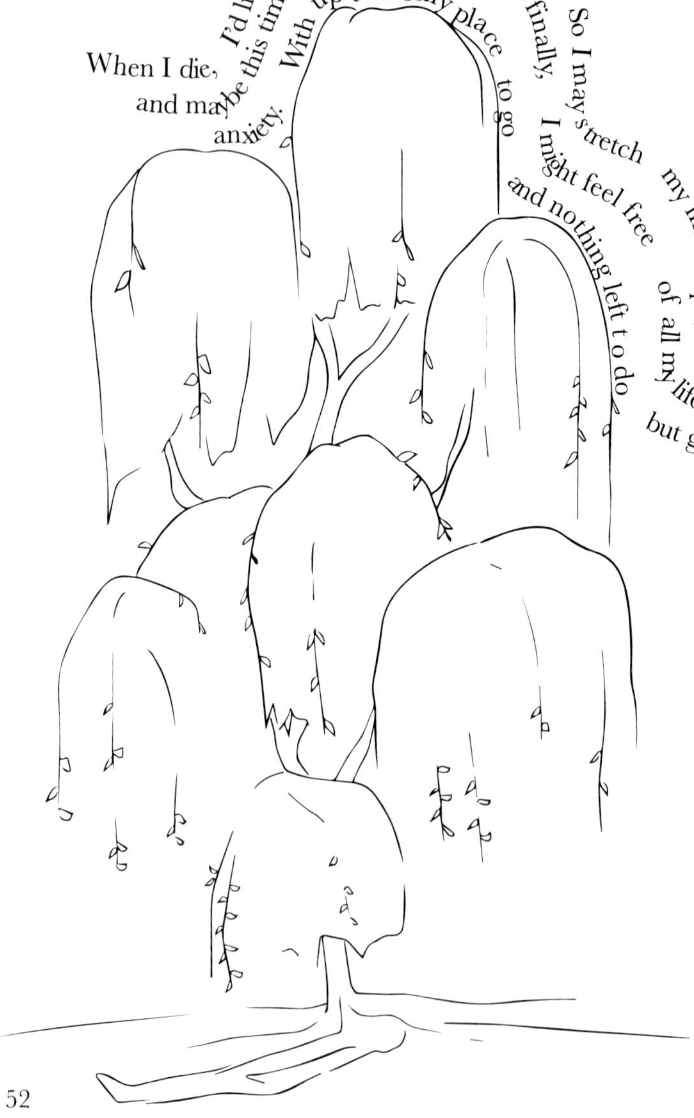

Why do I feel inferior
to every person
I have ever met,
and every person
I will ever meet?

I didn’t get to say goodbye,
but when I look up at the sky,
I see that twinkle from your eye
and know you never left.

‘Cause in those stars is where you said
you’d stitch a quilt and make your bed.
So any night I'm filled with dread
or falling deep into my head,
I’ll go outside
to see the sky
and know you never left.

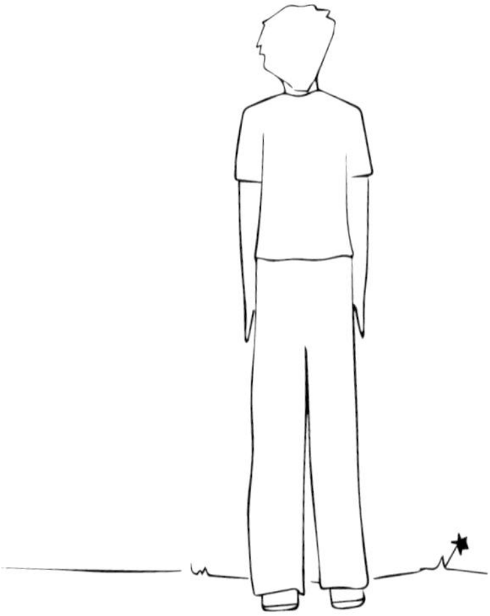

Love of my life

is not an honor
casually bestowed.

-things my grandma said

Your impatience is all that you left with me.

And now I must wait an eternity,

before I can see you again.

-thanks

They keep me up at night,

the spiders in my head,

that spin their webs

and lay their eggs

and crawl beneath my skin.

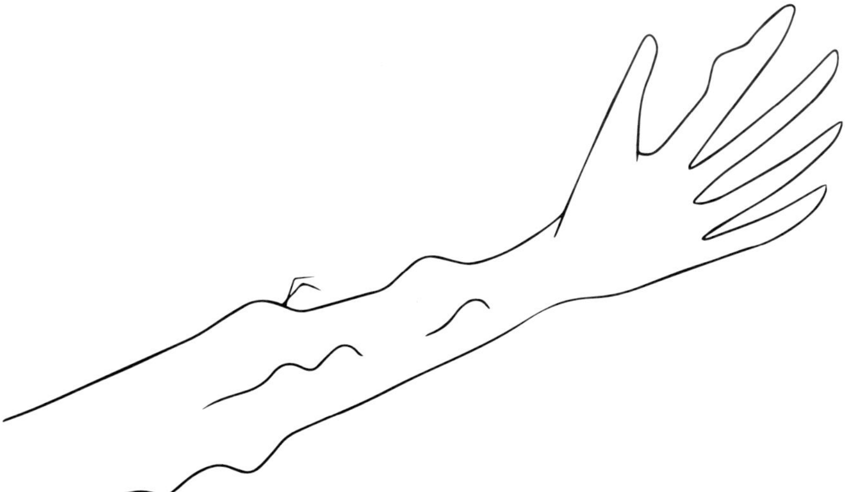

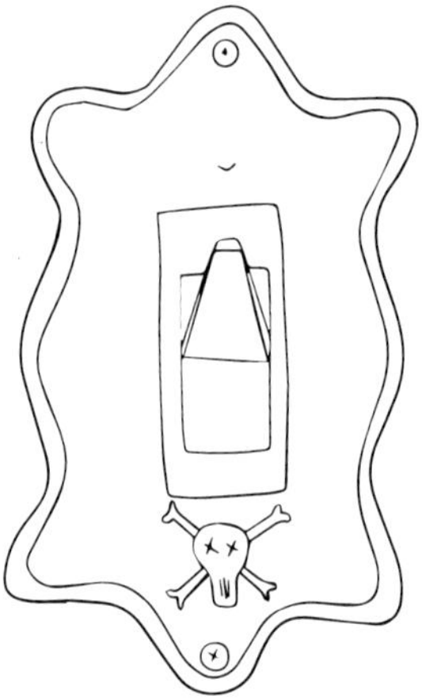

I feel like a light switch
flipping on and off.

Today I am bright,
full of passion and might,

but tomorrow
I'll wake up
to self-destruct,

and set fire to my life.

I search for secrets
in the air.
Beg my breaths,
the Ins and Outs,
to teach me
what it means
to be effortless.

I don't cry because
I never got to say goodbye.
I cry because you died,
and never knew the real me.
I never gave you the chance,
never introduced you two,
never took off the mask long enough for you
to gaze into his eyes or
cup his cheek in your hand.

Now I sit on this mountain
of nevers and what ifs
and wonder,
what you would have said to him,
what stories you'd have told,
the secrets you'd have shared,
or if maybe,
just maybe,
all along you saw him there,
but were too polite to pry.

Let it pass.

Let it run its course.

Every crashing wave
must recede,
and when it does,
you will feel air

fill up your lungs
and remember

you are alive.

I'm 6'1, so pretty tall,
but at this place I feel so small.

With every word I shrink an inch
because the small talk makes me
flinch.

I press my back against the wall
and soon I'm only two feet tall.

-I have fun at parties

You feel small the Universe whispers,

wrapping me up in her stars.

I nod.

Good. Now you may finally live.

I love sad songs,

not because I like being sad,
but because I like reminding myself

I am allowed
to feel.

I envy the courageous,
not the gladiators or giant slayers,
but the rare breed of people
who do not care
what others think of them.
Who are excited at the prospect
of a room full of strangers.
Those that can disarm you with a smile
because they are comfortably themselves,
because their eyes do not scan
your body for your weak spots,
their own flaws proudly pinned
down the trains of their ball gowns.
These people do not look at you,
they look for you,
into you,
without fear of judgement,
without needing to be liked.

That is the courage I envy.

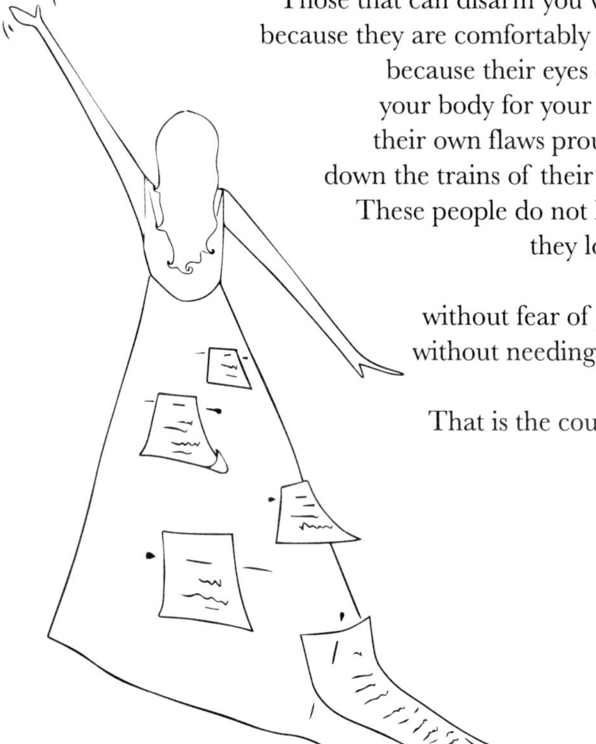

It’s impossible

to pick myself

up off this floor

when my hands

were the first

to shatter.

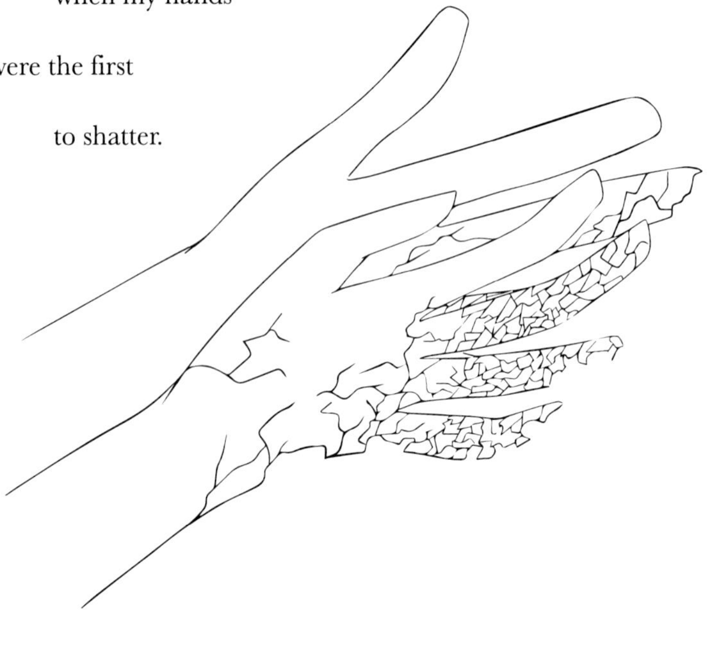

I cannot reach you
with my hands,

so I must reach you
with these words.

I crave quiet,

the silence of the sea,

to dive beneath my choppy thoughts,

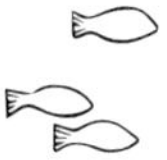

and sink down to tranquility.

They're just poems! my mind cries.
No one reads them! No one cares!

That is why I like them my heart whispers.
That is why they set us free.

You are in constant battle
with your own insignificance,

fighting a war
that billions have lost before you,

and billions will continue to lose
long after you are gone.

A tree does not fear toppling over

just because it cannot see its roots.

The most tragic superhero movie
is not the one where the hero dies,
or gets defeated by the villain.

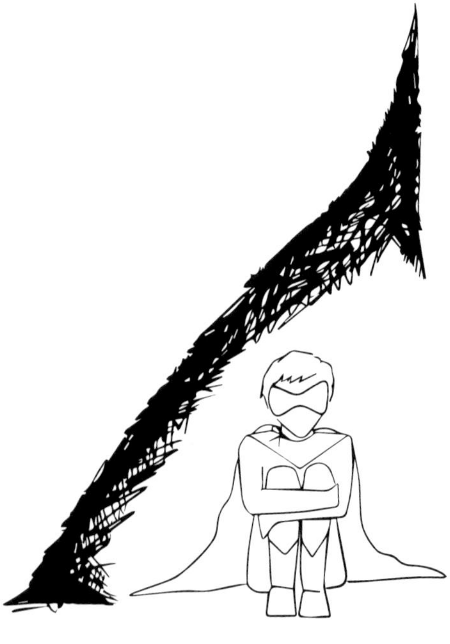

It is the one where the hero
defeats himself,
by discovering his powers
and being too afraid
to ever use them.

You keep your head in the clouds,

then complain when you can't see the ground.

Take off your shoes
and walk across
this patch of grass
so the Earth
may feel you on
her skin.

Still

your

mind

by

moving

your

body

Whenever I’m impatient
or feel weak,
I try to think of sidewalk trees,
how roots
don’t break through concrete
overnight.

Don't just give the homeless man
your dollar bill,
give him your humanity.

Ask him for his name,
shake his hand,
look into his eyes
just to say
I see you.

I saw a boy atop a hill,
just him and his balloon.
He raised his hand and let it go
without a trace of gloom.

I watched him watch it disappear
into a sky of grey.
Disturbed, I said, *Dear boy, but why?*
Why let it slip away?

He stared at me with vacant eyes,
unsure of what to do,
and then he pointed at the sky and said,
But that was you.

The potential, dreams, and hopes you had,
all when you were young.
You let them slip and drift away
and burn up in the sun.

Why do we live in a society that
treats our hopes and our dreams
like snake bites?
These poisonous desires that must
be sucked out and spit
into the dirt?

Why do we tell our children
they will grow up
to do whatever they want,
be whatever they want,
then do nothing but gawk
as the world
rips the magic carpet
right out from under them?
So they may replace it
with a lifeless, flat
welcome mat
to wipe their filthy boots on?

No.
Let us end that cycle.
Live up to our promises,
so those that escape this dull fate
who don't settle for a rat race,
are not just
the lucky few.
Let us wake the masses up
and show them
that hopes and dreams
are not venom in our veins,
but the marrow in our bones.

Fear
and doubt
are my
collar and
my chain.

I've been trained
to forget
I can walk
so much farther
without them.

Why is it the moment
I create something new
I am overwhelmed and distraught,
like I will never be able to do it again,
the well has dried,
and this poem in my hands
is my last?

(sigh)

Fuck.
Fuck fuck
fuck fuck fuck
fuck fuck fuck fuck.

FUCK.
Fuck.

(screams)
(bangs the steering wheel)
(sits)
(inhales)

(remembers he has food to eat,
a place to live, love from others)
(finds patience)
(exhales)
(turns on podcast)

(drives home)

-post day job dialogue

Death by coasting

I am ruined
by your
stubborn need
to succeed.

-a message from my art

I
am
a
puppet

whose
strings

are
made
from
others'
words.

They
pull
me
up,
and
down,
and
side
to
side,

drag
me
through
this
helpless
life.

One
day
I
hope

I'll
find
my
words

and
cut
these
strings
myself.

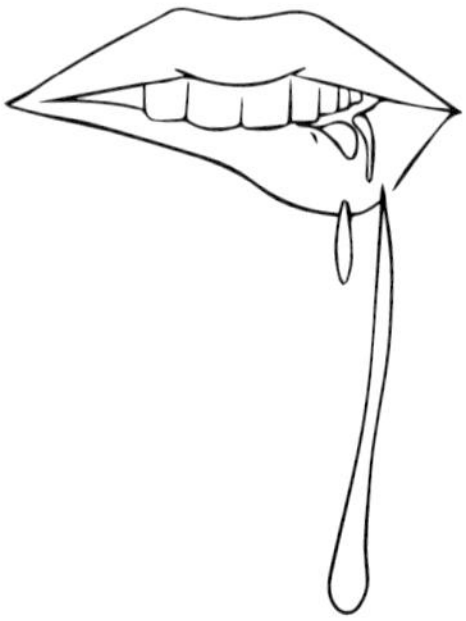

I am addicted
to the rush,
the highs,
how wide
my eyes
become
from those
sweet words.
They drip like
poisoned honey
off my lips.
Money? No, no.
I crave praise,
prefer sensation.
Willingly,
I pay the price
for my brain's vice,
that validation.

Why is it that

in my mind's sea,

the happy thoughts

just sink like rocks

and all those dark
and heavy thoughts,
they always float
right to the top?

You walk around feeling crushed
by uncertainty,
blindly searching for answers
that do not exist,
acting like you are the only one
who has ever experienced
this thing called life.

Open your eyes.

Sit down with your mother,
call your uncle, your aunt,
visit your grandparents.
They are treasure troves,
a wealth of wisdom.

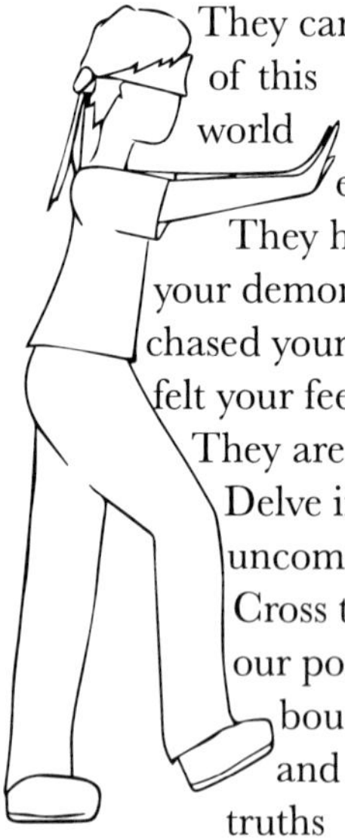

They carried the weight
of this
world long before you were
ever a part of it.
They have battled
your demons,
chased your dreams,
felt your feelings.
They are still feeling them.
Delve into the
uncomfortable.
Cross the divide,
our polite invisible
boundaries,
and seek out their
truths

for your own.

My, it is difficult to focus
on life
when death
is such an effortless
obsession.

Green Olives,

when I was a kid
I used to gag at the sight of you.
Hold my breath and plug my nose,
but now, somehow,
all grown up
you've seduced me.

Green olives,
you are my new love,
not just for your smooth
and salty taste,
but for your indelible proof
that we are all
inexplicably
ever-changing.

I used to cry at setting suns

but then I met

the moon.

You have your first love and then you have

your first love

Your lightning struck

and turned my heart

to ruby glass.

Please,

I beg,

don't break me.

I never believed
in *meant to be*

until my head
fit perfectly

between your chin
and your chest.

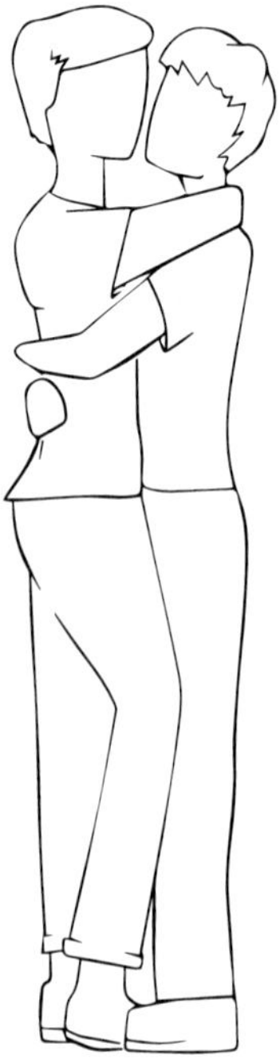

The world was bland and bleak

until you stepped into my life,

with those

kaleidoscopic
eyes,

and showed me all the color.

Does it turn you on?
How much power you have
over me? My body?
That with just one look
you can turn me to stone,
and another,
have me crumble
at your feet?

-my man is a Medusa

My entire world
begins and ends
in those
six inches
between our lips,
where we lie
face to face
on that pillow.

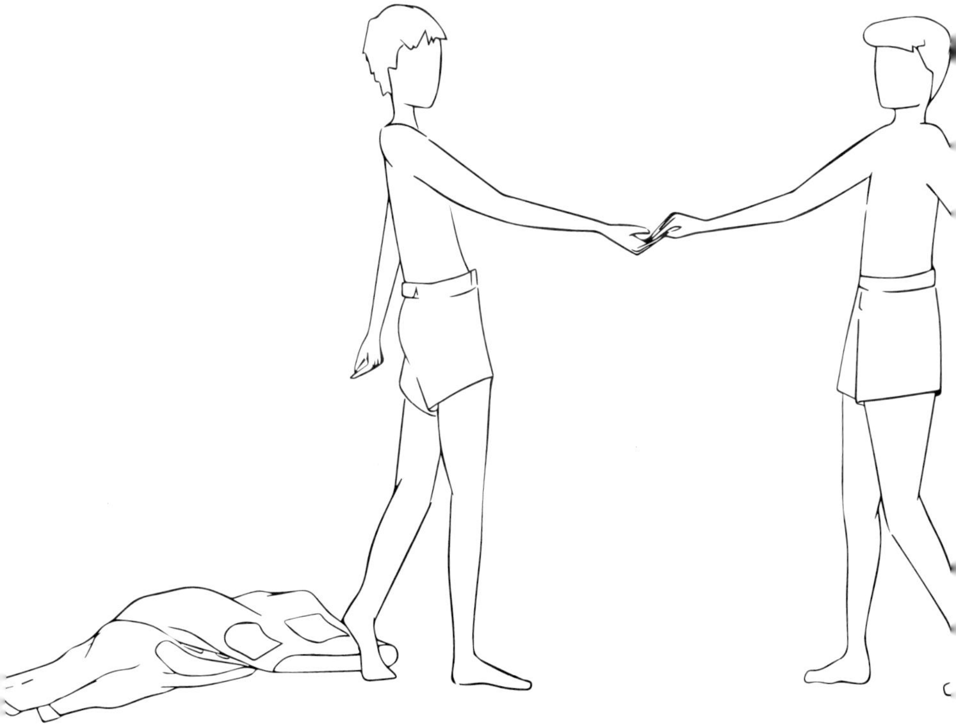

When

w e

are apart

I choke and gasp,

because my lungs

don't ask for air,

they beg

to breathe you in.

Before you,

I'd never felt the w e i g h t l e s s n e s s

never knew
the agony of sleepless nights
or what it's like

to melt

into another's skin.

Before you,
I didn't have a favorite sound,
but now,
when I lie on your bare chest,
I am lulled to sleep by the gentle hymn
of your beating heart.

You see treasure in my chest,
precious stones within my bones,
buried things I never knew
were even there.

I didn't know myself
before you.

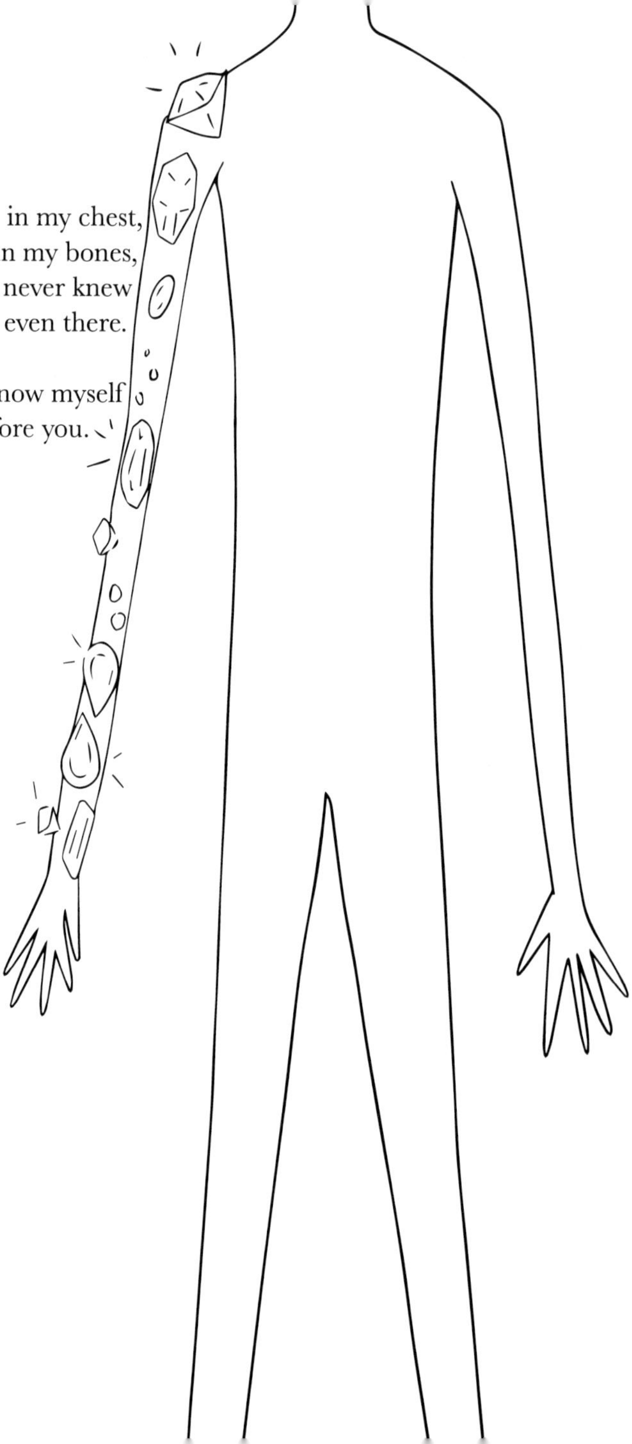

Tell me,

is it a blessing
or a tragedy,

if your first
love
is your last?

Do you remember that night?
Our red wine lips?
Those *I love yous*
on the tips
of our tongues?
The very first
of so many
to come?

You make everyone
around you
feel seen.

That
is your superpower.

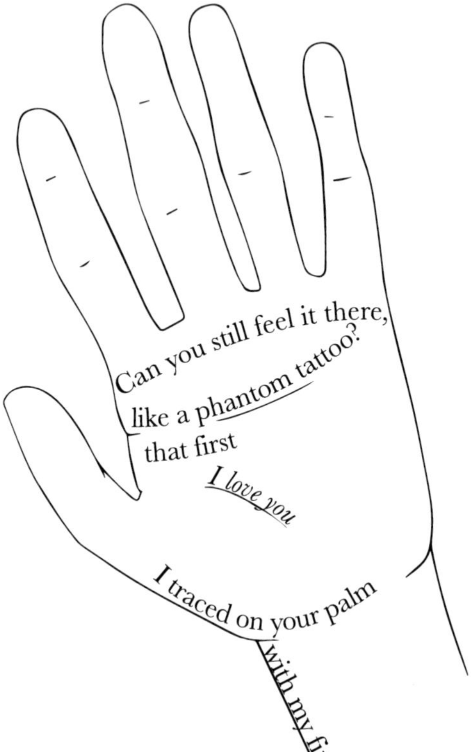
Can you still feel it there,
like a phantom tattoo?
that first
I love you
I traced on your palm
with my finger?

Will you always love me? you ask.
And I laugh,
because my love for you is everlasting,
a force of nature
as wide as the sky
and as deep as the sea.
Walk out in the sun
and feel the heat of my love
kiss your skin.
In every gust of wind,
feel my fingers through your hair.
Hear the bees hum your name
and the birds sing my words.
Every flower will bow at your feet.
For they worship our everlasting love.

Your smile is my paradise.

All day I wish
to lounge in its warmth,
like a hammock in the sun.

I need you
like the flowers need the rain.
I am thunder
calling out your name.
You electrify my body
when you light up this dark sky.
Your love so bright, so moving,
the clouds can't help but cry.

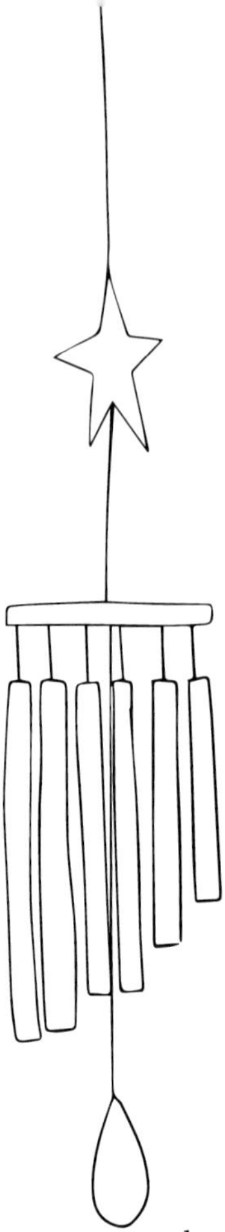

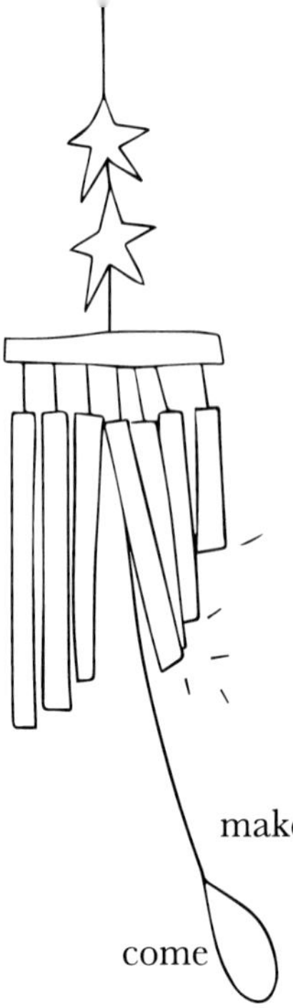

out of me.

make music

come

by your touch,

to be moved

long for breeze,

like windchimes

for you

I yearn

I hope

if I keep swimming
in your sea,

your gentle waves,

eventually,

will smooth out all
my roughness.

I am lost
in your eyes
and never felt
more at home.

A relationsh ip is a game
of tug of war

between two souls
wanting to be one,

but de sperate
not to change

he said,

and those heavy words,
they crushed me.

How long can I contain
the swirling sandstorm
in my brain?
This whipping, stinging,
blinding pain
that's swallowed
all my light.

I think
I'm falling
desperately
in love
with
hating myself.

Don't tell me that you think I'm good
'cause then I'll go and think I'm great,
a genius with some shiny fate,
whose head is far too large.

And in my new reality
if I don't reach divinity,
the crash and burn
will surely be
a devastating
end to me.

You have been hacked
by Self-Hatred,
who slithered through the backdoor
you left unlocked and open.
He infected your system,
placed you on auto,
while he dimmed your eyes,
muted your voice,
rewired your brain
so that any and all positive thoughts,
of self-worth,
of self-love,
would be filtered out and deleted.
He took control without you even
knowing
and now he will change your very code
until you are
unrecognizable.

You feel helpless,
hopeless,
out of control,
but like any virus
there is always a cure.
It is in your breath.
It is in the silence of a room,
where you can quiet your mind,
where you will slow,
and reflect,
and reset
your system.

You are / have always been / my world.

But will there / even be / a trace of me / if my world ends?

I hate how often
you say that
you're proud of me.

I hate that I hate that.

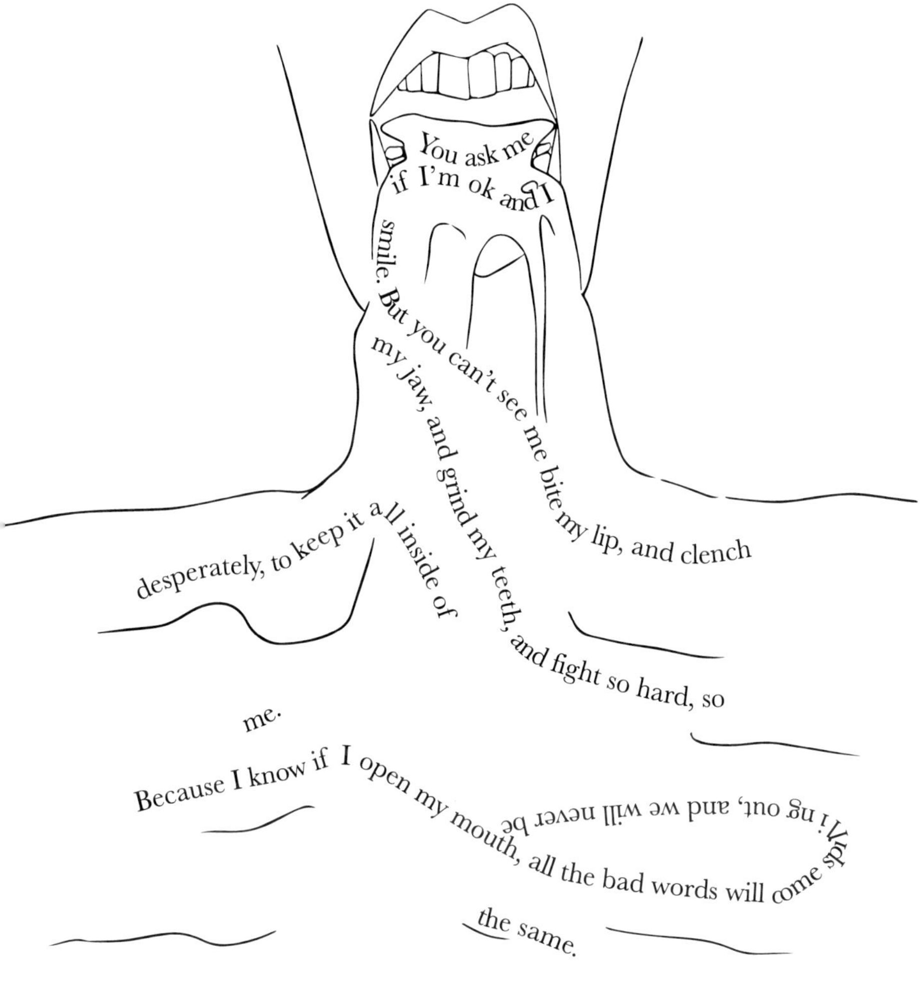

You ask me if I'm ok and I smile. But you can't see me bite my lip, and clench my jaw, and grind my teeth, and fight so hard, so desperately, to keep it all inside of me.

Because I know if I open my mouth, all the bad words will come spilling out, and we will never be the same.

Maybe if I stay away,
you won't catch

this sadness.

I take cold showers
to wake me up,
to wash you off my skin,
not because I do not like you on my skin,
but because sometimes
I need to remember
how it feels
to be myself.

So often I compare the air in this room with myself, used, but unseen.

There is nothing louder
than the sound
of your silence.

When I look in the mirror,
I no longer see myself.
Only you.
Your eyes.
Your lips.
The dimples
from your cheeks.
I am lost.
I have let myself,
erase myself.

You don’t fear death,
you’re just afraid
to lose control.

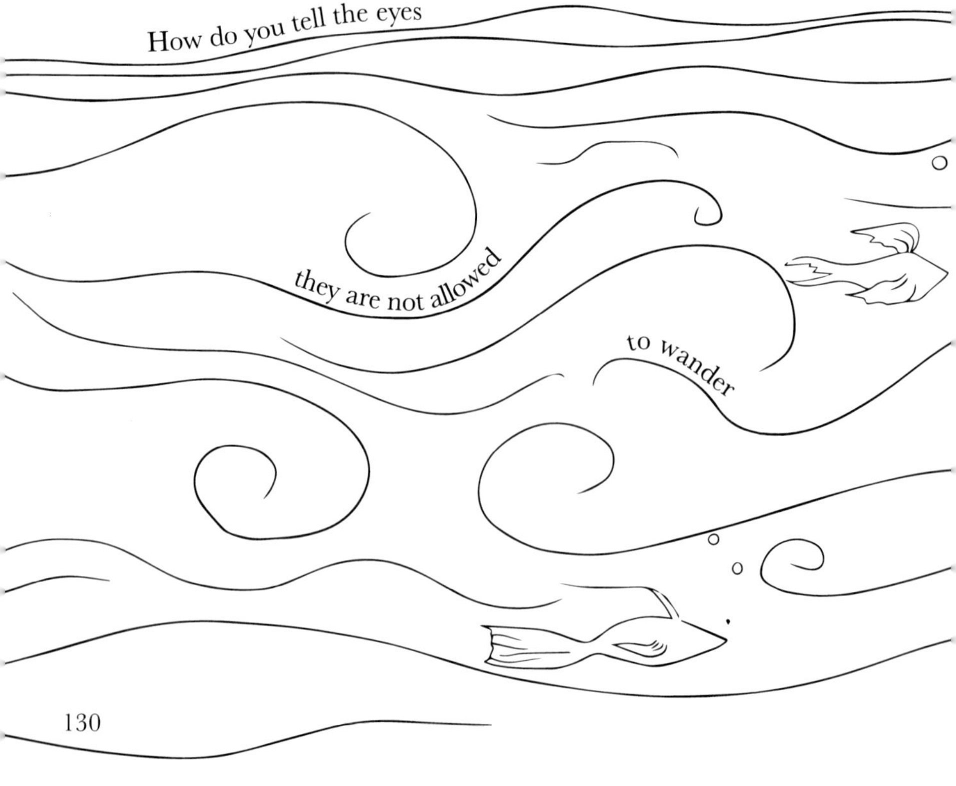
How do you tell the eyes
they are not allowed
to wander

when your thoughts
get to cross
all seven seas?

Like static in a shirt,
I cling to you,
to the idea of you,
to the hope of us,
to your version of my future.

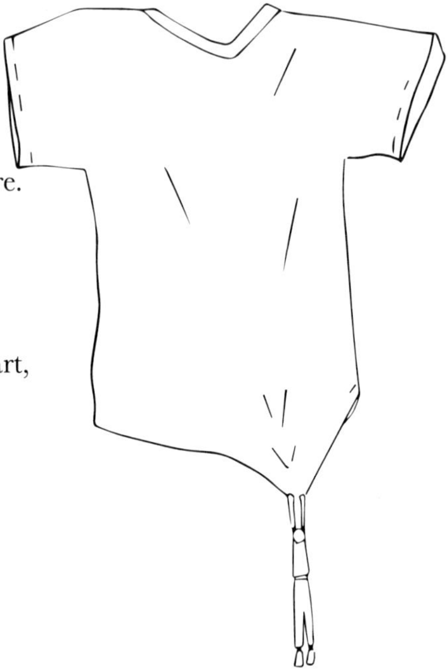

I cling,
desperately,
because I am afraid.
Not of us being ripped apart,
but of the guilt,
of the devastation
I will feel
if my static ever fades,
and slowly,
uncontrollably,
I just
peel off
from you
and
fall
away.

Are you a cruel person
if the only person
you are cruel to
is you?

Please,
just look away.
I cannot bear
to see your eyes,
your face
witnessing
this
fall from grace.
My own
undoing.

I smile,
and I laugh,

but look
into my eyes

and you will see
I am

bursting

at the seams.

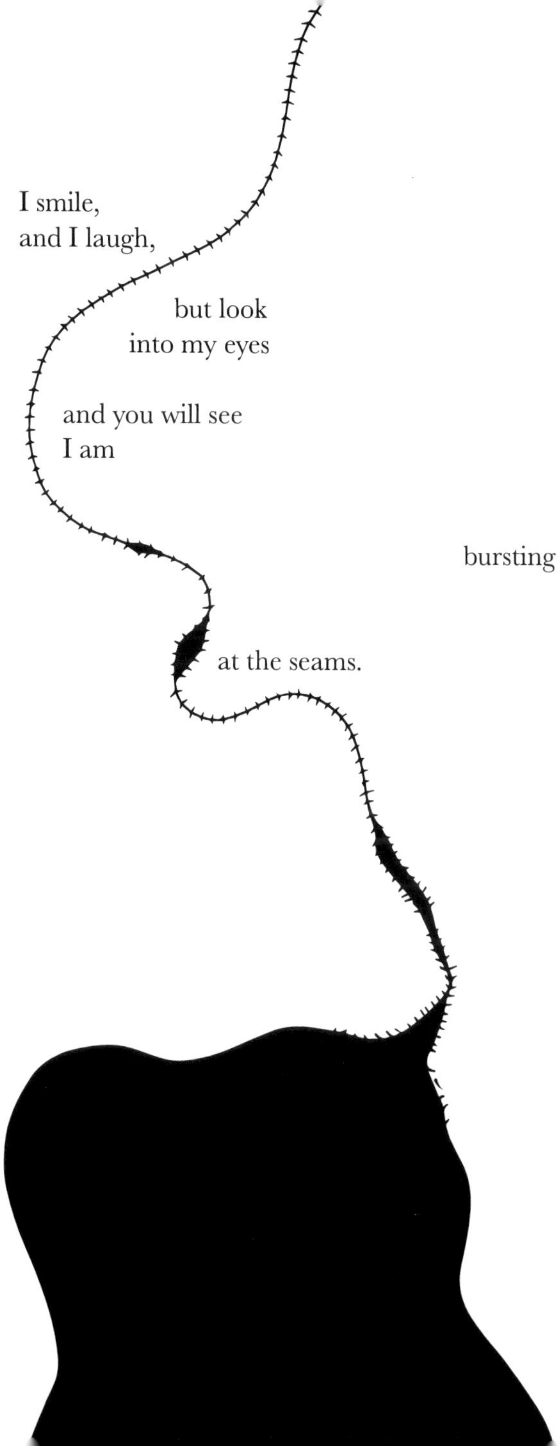

My favorite thing about you
is your light.

How even in my darkest night
your goodness shines and glows.

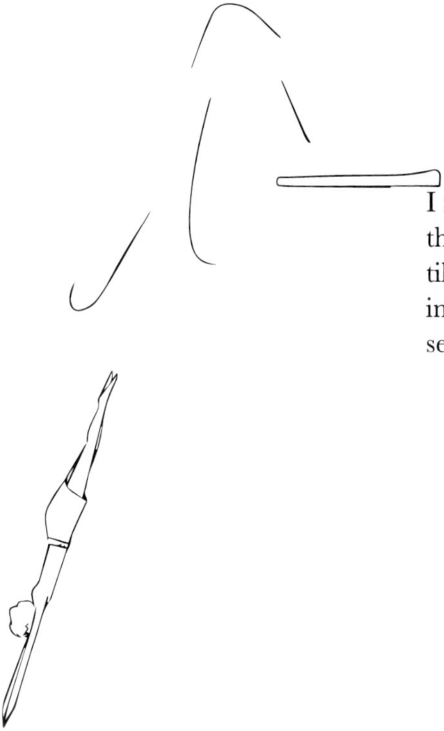

I never knew
that I could float
till I dove
in those
sea green eyes.

Lost at sea,
he guides me home.

My lover
is a lighthouse.

This is stupid.
This is dumb.
I'm not having
any fun.
All these poems
simply are
a waste of time.

But then again,
when I rhyme,
it's the only time
I shine,
'cause these stupid,
silly words,
though they're dumb,
they're all mine.

So yes, I'll write.
Just write and write,
and when frustration comes
I'll fight
the urge to pack my things
and go,
'cause who knows what
these poems might grow.

How do you do it? I ask.

Do what? the volcano bellows.

Keep your faith I reply,
sifting my hand through her rocky soil.
You cannot see the lava inside you,
yet you still believe someday you will erupt.

The ground quakes.
There is no need to see she chuckles,
if you can feel a fire burning in your belly.

Poems are like fireflies in mid-July,
blinking through a dimming sky.
They're hard to catch,
but when you do,
oh that glow
does dazzle you.

Who cares
if no one reads it,
no one buys it.

It only matters
how it feels
in your hands.

A message to the dreamer,
to the artist and the rebel,
to those that crave more:

Sometimes the weight of the world,
of our existence,
of our endless emotional turmoil,
leaves us numb.

So we may look like we are sleepwalking
through this crowd
but look close enough
and you will see
we are the only ones
awake.

The only ones letting the world in
and ourselves out,
feeling our feelings,
not pretending,
not walking down this street
like life is easy,
like everything is fine
and the world is good.

Sure, it is taxing,
the endless heartache,
the anxiety,
the longing.
But wouldn't you rather feel and die,
than lie to live
and never feel at all?? ? ??

To save the world:

All
Men
Must
~~Die~~
Cry

Maybe you won't change the world.
Maybe you'll be perfectly content
just appreciating
the many wonders
that are already here.

We are two trees growing
side by side,
and though our branches
intertwine,
our leaves
must stay our own.

If you are ever to be truly happy
in your life,
in your relationship,
you must get to the point where you can
look straight into the eyes of
your deepest love,
the love of your life,
and think to yourself
I do not need him.
Of course, you would cry a sea of tears
if he ever left.
He is the sweetness you crave,
your patch of sun on a cloudy day,
forever and always,
you will want him.
But you do not need him.
You are independent,
secure,
capable on your own.
Not half a heart
but whole,
so drill that deep
into your bones
because that
is self-love.
That
is the secret
to a healthy
relationship.
The only way
together forever,
ever works.

You seem to think
there is this perfect You out there,
somewhere down the line,
patiently waiting
at your final stop.
This be-all, end-all, You,
who has every answer,
every meaning to life,
all the keys to success
neatly strung on a loop.

But you know it's untrue.
A fantasy to help you sleep.
A lie to tell yourself
when your feet scream from all the walking,
when your hands bleed from all the building.
You imagine and pretend
because you cannot face the fact
that your road is endless.
You have no finish line.
You are a work in perpetual progress.

There will always be another coat to paint,
more bricks to lay,
future drafts you will crumple up
and throw away.
You will never feel at ease,
never know it all,
and most definitely never
have it all.

But do not despair.
Do not let the thought of all means and no end
weigh you down.
No, let it lift you up,
excite you,
inspire you,
free you from the unobtainable.
You never have to settle.
You'll never be bored.
It is never too late.
So let your beaten mind and body
soak in comfort
knowing there will never be a perfect You
but you,
can always be better.

Even the most magnificent

fields of flowers
all begin

quite humbly

from a single, tiny seed,
in a strange and barren plot,

with nobody,

with nothing

but the courage

to put down roots

and the hope
to bloom.

These poems are not good.

They are not bad.

They simply,

unequivocally,

are.

The only thing
I want to achieve
in my life
is the serene
acceptance
of my death.

In a field in Minnesota,
we felt the grass beneath our feet,
the woody air fill up our lungs,
the dipping sun rays kiss our cheeks.

We listened to the gentle wind,
which rustled trees, so tall.
We didn’t have to say a word.
The birds, they sang them all.

Who would have thought
that time could stop
on a family walk with Koda.
I think I found
the meaning of life
in a field in Minnesota.

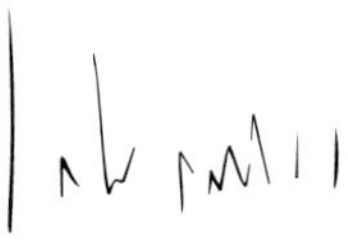

Cycles
Endless
Cycles

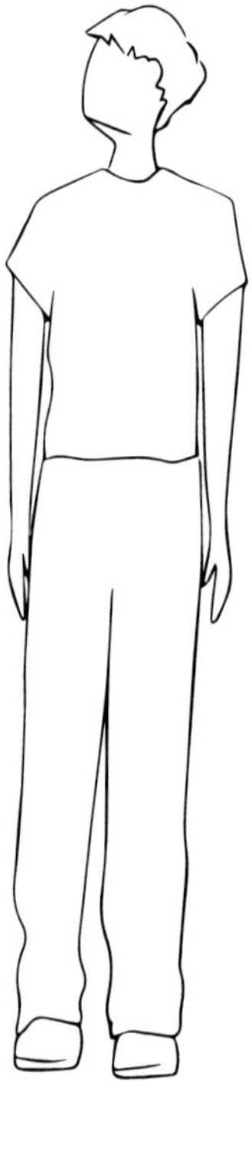

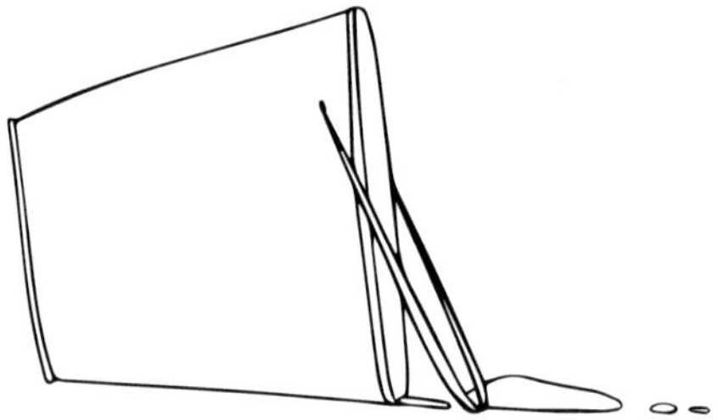

Grant Chemidlin is a poet and screenwriter living in Los Angeles. *He Felt Unwell (So He Wrote This)* is his first published collection. Follow him on Instagram @grantcpoetry for more.

Alexandra Lenihan is an illustrator and writer living in Los Angeles. You can find her illustrated memoir, *The First Two Months,* and her blog at www.len1010.com. You can find her instagram @len.10.10

Made in United States
North Haven, CT
06 February 2023

32122339R00098